Silly Goose's BIG Story

KEIKO KASZA

SCHOLASTIC INC.

For Mikey McMullen and Isaiah Stroup, our friends always

ISBN 978-0-545-82121-6

Copyright © 2012 by Keiko Kasza. All rights reserved.
Published by Scholastic Inc., 557 Broadway, New York, NY 10012,
by arrangement with G. P. Putnam's Sons, a division of Penguin Young Readers Group,
a member of Penguin Group (USA) LLC, A Penguin Random House Company.
SCHOLASTIC and associated logos are trademarks and/or registered trademarks of Scholastic Inc.

12 11 10 9 8 7 6 5 4 3 2 1   14 15 16 17 18 19/0

Printed in the U.S.A.   40

First Scholastic printing, November 2014

Design by Marikka Tamura
Text set in Mushmellow
The art was done in gouache on three-ply bristol illustration paper.

Goose made up great stories.
His friends would always beg him,
"Tell us a story, Goose!"

One day, Goose said, "Once upon a time, there were fierce pirates!"

Soon they were sailing the seven seas together, looking for treasures. And Goose was the captain, the fiercest of all.

Another day, Goose said, "Once upon a time, there were scary dinosaurs!"

Soon they were roaming the earth together, hunting and growling. And naturally, Goose was the T. rex, the scariest of all.

Then another day, Goose said, "Once upon a time, there was a mighty king!"

Soon they were marching through towns and hills together, conquering the world.

And who got to play the king, the mightiest of all?
Why, Goose, of course.

"Wait a minute, Goose," said Beaver. "You always play the hero. Why can't we take turns?"

"Yeah," said Porcupine. "I'd like to be the hero sometime!"

"Me, too," said Squirrel.

"No way," said Goose.

"I always play the hero.
Come on, keep marching!"

"That's selfish," said his friends.

But Goose wouldn't give in. "They are my stories, so I'm the hero!" he insisted.

They were so busy arguing, they didn't notice that someone was listening.

Suddenly, a big wolf shouted,

Hello,

lunch!

They all screamed and ran, but poor Goose tripped
on his royal cape. Wolf scooped him up in an instant.

"So, you're the hero, huh?" Wolf chuckled.
"More like a hero sandwich to me!"
Goose was in big trouble. He had to think fast.
Finally he had an idea. "Mr. Wolf," Goose said,
"I'm glad I found you. You're in great danger."
"Is that so?" Wolf laughed. "How?"
"Well, I'll tell you!"

Goose began the biggest story
he ever told. "Once upon a time,
there were thousands of happy
wolves living on this mountain."
"Uh-huh," said Wolf.

"Then one day, umm . . . what's his name?
Oh, yeah, Wem showed up," said Goose.
"Wem? Who's that?"
"Oh, Wem is short for Wolf-Eating Monster."

Goose continued. "He used to wander around saying, 'Yum, yum, I smell a wolf.' And when he found one, he popped it into his mouth like a peanut."

"You are lying!" said Wolf, but he looked worried. "It's true, Mr. Wolf," said Goose. "Do you see thousands of wolves here? And this is the worst part— Wem is back!"

Just at that moment . . .

. . . the trees started to shake and they
heard loud footsteps in the distance.
"What's that?" said Wolf.

Soon, spikes of hair appeared
above the treetops.
   "It couldn't be!" said Wolf.

Then a deep voice bellowed,

YUM, YUM, I smell a wolf...

"It's Wem!" cried Wolf. He dropped Goose like a hot potato and took off running. He never looked back.

"Whew!" Goose was relieved, but not for long. Something big was coming his way. It was getting closer and closer.

Then, from behind the trees there came . . .

. . . his ferocious-looking friends.

"Yum, yum, I smell a wolf." They were still growling together.

Goose shouted with relief, "Oh, you guys! You're Wem!"

"Yup! I shook the trees," said Squirrel.

"The footsteps were me, slapping my tail," said Beaver.

"I was Wem's hair," said Porcupine.

"Hey, you know what?!" Beaver shouted
suddenly. "We finally got to play the heroes."
"*Play* the heroes?!" cried Goose.
"You **ARE** the heroes. You saved me!"

"Tell us another story, Goose!" the friends begged as they walked home.

"Okay, I've got a good one," said Goose.
"Once upon a time, there was a silly Goose
who had the three greatest friends in
the world . . ."